USBORNE FIRST READING
Level One

USBORNE FIRST READING

The **Fox** and the **Crow**

Retold by Mairi Mackinnon
Illustrated by Rocio Martinez

Retold by Lesley Sims
Illustrated by Elisa Squillace

USBORNE FIRST READING

The **Lion** and the **Mouse**

Retold by Mairi Mackinnon
Illustrated by Frank Endersby

USBORNE FIRST READING

The **Sun** and the **Wind**

Retold by Mairi Mackinnon
Illustrated by Francesca di Chiara

On the Farm

Susanna Davidson

Illustrated by
Alessandra Roberti

Reading consultant: Alison Kelly
Roehampton University

This story is about two children,

Lily and Ben.

There are also hens,

sheep

and cows.

Lily and Ben live
on a farm.

The sun rises...

and the rooster wakes
them up.

cock-a-doodle-doo!

Lily and Ben
rush outside.

MOO!

8

The cows are coming.

It's milking time.

A huge tanker takes
the milk away.

Now, it's time to feed the hens.

peck-peck-peck

13

Lily goes into the
henhouse.

Outside, the sheep are
in the large field.

Ben counts them.
"Oh no!" he cries.

"A sheep is missing."

19

The sheep isn't in
the corn field.

She isn't in the garden.

Where can she be?

She's in the barn...

with three baby lambs.

Puzzles

Puzzle 1

Can you match the animals
to their babies?

hen

lambs

sheep

kittens

cat

chicks

Puzzle 2

Find these things in the picture:

geese   dog   roof   sun

rooster   grass

Puzzle 3

Can you spot the differences
between these two pictures?

There are eight to find.

Answers to puzzles

Puzzle 1

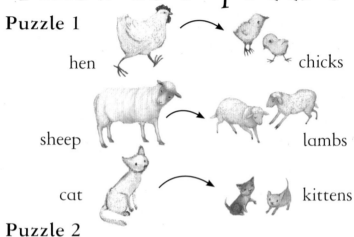

hen   chicks

sheep   lambs

cat   kittens

Puzzle 2

roof

rooster   sun

dog

geese   grass

Puzzle 3

Based on a story by Anna Milbourne
Series editor: Lesley Sims
Designed by Emily Bornoff
Digital manipulation by Nick Wakeford

This edition first published in 2011 by Usborne Publishing Ltd.,
Usborne House, 83-85 Saffron Hill, London EC1N 8RT, England.
www.usborne.com Copyright © 2011, 2006 Usborne Publishing Ltd.

USBORNE FIRST READING
Level Two

Retold by Lesley Sims
Illustrated by Georgien Overwater

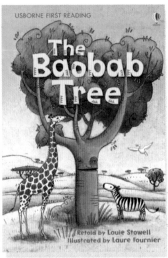

Retold by Louie Stowell
Illustrated by Laure Fournier

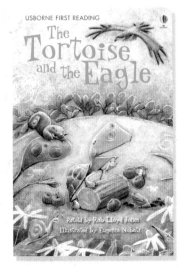

Retold by Rob Lloyd Jones
Illustrated by Eugenia Nobati

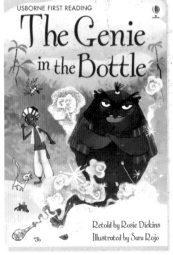

Retold by Rosie Dickins
Illustrated by Sara Rojo